Decepticon™ Attack!

written by Michael Teitelbaum
illustrated by MVCreations

Reader's Digest Children's Books™

Pleasantville, New York • Montréal, Québec • Bath, United Kingdom

An ancient war between the Transformers—robots with the ability to change their bodies into vehicles—had raged on for millions of years. The battle between good Transformers called Autobots and evil Transformers called Decepticons had started on the robots' home planet, Cybertron. It now moved to planet Earth.

On Earth's moon, Megatron, leader of the Decepticons, had set up a fortress. From here, he planned to wage war against the Autobots, who had established a base on Earth.

Megatron looked up into the star-filled sky and shook his fist angrily. "The time has come to pay a visit to the Autobots!" he shouted. "We will crush the Autobots, then take over planet Earth.

Megatron hurried through his fortress, arriving at the control room. There he joined his fellow Decepticons—Cyclonus, Demolishor, and Starscream. The four stood in front of a huge video screen, watching as images of Earth's mightiest military vehicles flashed by.

"We must select our vehicle forms for the coming attack on Earth," Megatron ordered.

"These are the most powerful military vehicles on Earth," Demolishor explained.

"Excellent," replied Megatron. "It's time to choose our vehicles!"

"I choose that one!" said Starscream, Megatron's second-in-command. He pointed at the image of a jet fighter streaking through the sky, blasting tanks and other vehicles below.

"I select that vehicle," said Demolishor, looking at a video of a missile tank rumbling along rough terrain, blasting a truck. Demolishor was a loyal veteran who had stood at Megatron's side in countless battles.

"And I pick that flying vehicle!" Cyclonus declared, pointing at pictures of an army helicopter moving swiftly through the air. The helicopter fired missiles at a building on the ground. Trigger-happy Cyclonus was always ready for a fight.

"I will assume the form of that vehicle!" Megatron announced, staring at the image of a huge super tank. The tank's enormous guns were blasting a jet fighter in the sky.

"We are now prepared to launch our attack against the Autobots and their leader, Optimus Prime!" Megatron bellowed.

On Earth, three friends rode along a bumpy mountain road. Twelve-year-old Rad was pedaling his BMX bike. Ten-year-old Carlos raced along on his skateboard. Eleven-year-old Alexis followed on her scooter. The bike, skateboard, and scooter may have looked normal, but these were no ordinary vehicles. They were, in fact, Mini-cons, a long-lost type of Transformer from the planet Cybertron. The kids had discovered the Mini-cons in a mountain cave, and each had bonded with one of the little robots. The three kids had also met and made friends with the Autobots.

"I can't wait to see Optimus Prime again!" said Carlos, as he balanced on Grindor, his Mini-con skateboard.

"Maybe this time he'll let us help fight those Decepticon creeps," Alexis said hopefully, as she steered Sureshock, her Mini-con scooter.

"This is no game," Rad pointed out, as he pedaled High Wire, his Mini-con BMX bike. "This is a war!"

The three kids soon found Optimus Prime and two of his fellow Autobots, Hot Shot and Red Alert.

Carlos spun to a stop, kicking up his skateboard and snatching it out of the air with his hand. Grindor and the other two Mini-cons quickly transformed into their robot modes.

"Hey," Carlos said to Optimus Prime, "What are you guys up to?"

Optimus Prime turned to the children. "We are choosing our vehicle forms to aid us in our next battle with the Decepticons," he explained. "I have chosen that vehicle." Optimus Prime said, as he gazed at a large, powerful-looking tractor trailer on the highway below.

"And I have selected that vehicle," Hot Shot said, looking at a speeding yellow sports car.

"I will transform into that vehicle," Red Alert announced, staring intently at an armored rescue vehicle.

Without warning, the air around the Autobots and the children began to shimmer. A purple glow filled the sky. Then three figures appeared as the glow faded away.

"Megatron!" roared Optimus Prime.

"So we meet again, Optimus Prime," Megatron replied. "Only this time, victory will be mine!"

Megatron turned to the three children and their Mini-cons. "I see you have brought us a prize!" Megatron shouted. "Not only will we destroy the Autobots, but we will take these Mini-cons, as well!"

Mini-cons increased the power of all Transformers—Autobots and Decepticons alike. Upon seeing High Wire, Grindor, and Sureshock, Megatron decided to make them his.

"So it begins," he said. "Decepticons, TRANSFORM!"

"TRANSFORM!" Starscream echoed.

As the others watched, Starscream transformed into his vehicle mode. When the transformation was complete, he had taken on the form of a jet fighter plane.

"TRANSFORM!" Demolishor said.

He swiftly changed into a missile tank.

"TRANSFORM!" Cyclonus yelled.

Then he transformed into an army helicopter.

"TRANSFORM!" Megatron bellowed.

The Autobots looked on in horror as the Decepticon leader transformed into a giant super tank.

We must also change into our vehicle forms," Optimus Prime said. "Autobots, TRANSFORM!"

"With pleasure!" Red Alert agreed. "TRANSFORM!"

Instantly, Red Alert changed from his robot mode into an armored rescue vehicle.

"Don't forget about me!" Hot Shot added. "TRANSFORM!"

Hot Shot transformed into his vehicle mode, changing into a sleek yellow sports car.

Finally, Optimus Prime joined the others.

"TRANSFORM!" he shouted.

The ground shook as the Autobot leader changed from his robot form into his vehicle mode. He transformed into a huge tractor-trailer truck with a powerful engine.

Rad, Carlos, and Alexis stared at the transformations in stunned amazement.

"That's the coolest thing I've ever seen!" Carlos exclaimed.

"I think our Mini-cons are pretty cool," Alexis said defensively.

"And I think it would be smart for us to get into a safe hiding place before the real fighting begins!" Rad added.

"*Breedoooop,*" High Wire chirped in agreement.

Moving quickly, the three friends and their Mini-cons ducked into a nearby cave.

WHOOSH!

Starscream in his jet form and Cyclonus in his helicopter mode took to the air. Aiming their weapons, they unleashed a blistering barrage of machine-gun fire right at Optimus Prime!

"How do you like our tag team aerial attack, Optimus Prime?" Starscream asked mockingly.

Racing along with blinding speed, Red Alert
zoomed in front of Optimus Prime. The bullets from
the Decepticons' weapons bounced harmlessly off his
armor plating.

"Thanks, Red Alert," called Optimus Prime.

"Anytime, boss," replied Red Alert.

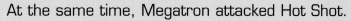

At the same time, Megatron attacked Hot Shot.

"Your puny little vehicle is no match for Decepticon power, Autobot!" Megatron said as he slammed into the speeding form of Hot Shot.

WHAM!

Megatron rammed him again, pushing Hot Shot toward the edge of a huge cliff. Hot Shot spun out of control, bouncing along the rugged terrain.

"I've got to stop before I'm pushed right over the edge!" Hot Shot exclaimed, slamming on his brakes. He skidded to a stop just inches from the cliff.

"We're outnumbered!" said Optimus Prime. "I must transform again, this time into Super Optimus Prime!"

As the leader of the Autobots, Optimus Prime had a special power, which only his closest teammates knew of. He had the ability to transform into a gigantic robot, incorporating his vehicle form into his huge body.

Optimus Prime began to grow, sprouting enormous arms and legs. When the transformation was complete, he towered over the Decepticons.

"You will not get your hands on those Mini-cons!" Super Optimus Prime declared. Then he reached down and swatted Megatron away as if he were an insect. Megatron could see that he and the Decepticons were no match for Super Optimus Prime.

"Retreat!" shouted Megatron, as he and the other Decepticons changed back into their robot forms. "We must return to our base on the moon. But I promise you, we will be back to fight another day!"

Then Megatron, Demolishor, Cyclonus, and Starscream vanished in a blinding purple flash.

After the Decepticons had gone, Rad, Carlos, Alexis, and their Mini-cons crept out of their hiding place.

"Are any of you hurt?" Optimus Prime asked, as he and his fellow Autobots returned to their normal robot forms.

"No way!" said Carlos. "You sure showed those guys who is boss."

"We have not seen the last of Megatron and the Decepticons, I'm afraid," Optimus Prime said.

"But you'll be ready when they come back," Alexis said confidently.

"And we'll be right here to help you!" Rad added, smiling.